NINJA CAMP

by Sue Fliess
Illustrated by Jen Taylor

RP|KIDS
PHILADELPHIA

**For my ninja agent, Jennifer.
–S. F.**

Running Press Kids
Hachette Book Group
1290 Avenue of the Americas, New York, NY 10104
www.runningpress.com/rpkids
@RP_Kids

Printed in China

First Edition: January 2019

Published by Running Press Kids, an imprint of Perseus Books, LLC,
a subsidiary of Hachette Book Group, Inc.The Running Press Kids name and logo
is a trademark of the Hachette Book Group.

The Hachette Speakers Bureau provides a wide range of authors for speaking events.
To find out more, go to www.hachettespeakersbureau.com or call (866) 376-6591.

The publisher is not responsible for websites (or their content)
that are not owned by the publisher.

Print book cover and interior design by T.L. Bonaddio

Library of Congress Control Number: 2018935974

ISBNs: 978-0-7624-6331-2 (hardcover), 978-0-7624-6330-5 (ebook),
978-0-7624-9304-3 (ebook), 978-0-7624-9305-0 (ebook)

1010

10 9 8 7 6 5 4 3 2 1

Through these woods, beyond the stream,
is where you'll join your ninja team.

"Will you teach us what you do?
So we can all be ninjas, too?"

"Patience, campers. Trust in me.
Ninja warriors soon you'll be.

You must practice every move.
Day by day, you will improve.
Are you fierce and unafraid?

"Yes! We'll try our very best
to master every ninja test!"

Stealthy ninjas must be sly,
build up strength, and learn to spy.

Creep in silence.

Move with speed.

THE NINJA CREED

Ninjas must be nimble, strong,

Choosing right instead

of wrong. Fight with honor

and respect, Using skill

and intellect. Walk the path

of truth and light—Become the

Ninjas of the Night!

Hide in shadows. Leave no trace.
Be prepared to flee or chase.

Ninjas run without a sound—
hover inches off the ground.

Blending in is your disguise.
Take the bad guys by surprise.

Timing is your best defense.
Trust your inner ninja sense.

"The rival camp may test our wills.

Use your newfound ninja skills.

Yikes! The Shadow Blade is gone!

Catch those Ninjas of the Dawn!"

Keep all targets
in your sight.
Wait until the
moment's right.

Jump across, then dive and flip . . .

Whoops! They just escaped your grip!

Trust your gut.

Stay in control.

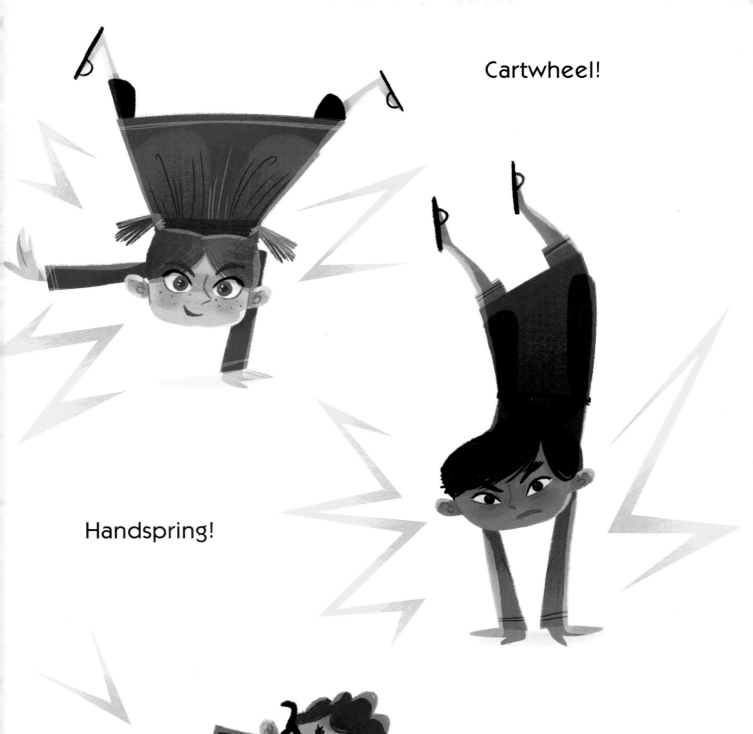

Cartwheel!

Handspring!

Drop and roll!

Duck their punches.

Dodge their kicks.

Trap them with your ninja sticks!"